Worth the Wood

By Dollyah Deering

"If someone must be great why not you?
And if you plan to be great why wait
Fore however is a dream to come true
If it isn't out into action when you wake?"

-Doe the Deer

This Book is Dedicated to
Tiara- Michelle, Rachel,
River-Jordan,
and YOU!

Legend has it sometime back,
there was a famous lumberjack.
He chopped a tree with axe in hand
that built the town right where we stand.

Living then was solely made
by lumbering and harvest trade.
Men chopped trees like mining gold
So they'd have wood that could be sold.

They'd go in groups and quickly scout,
the easiest tree to chop and carry out.
But one lumberjack ran off the path,
and found a tree he had to have.

Deeply rooted and tall it stood,
alone somehow in the middle of the wood.
He called the men, "Come, look and see!
I have found the perfect chopping tree!"

But when the men came, to their surprise,
was the biggest tree they've ever seen in their lives.
They grabbed their axes and chopped and chopped,
hours passed but the tree didn't drop.

Finally, the men all sit,
and tell the lumberjack, "We all quit.
This day's been wasted! It's not budging!
We've been gone all day and we're
bringing home nothing!"

The lumberjack said, "It's not all sorrow.
Let's just come back and try tomorrow."
But they did not come back. Only he
would return every day to chop at that tree.

Seasons changed and many months passed.
The men would all gather to watch and laugh.
"Give up lumberjack can't you see?
You're never going to chop that tree."

But the lumberjack ignored their talking
and everyday he just kept on chopping.
Then finally, with one, loud crack,
the mighty tree fell on its back.

And just as the lumberjack planned,
the tree behind it did also land,
and the tree after that and so on,
until there was a clearing a mile long.

The men were amazed and the lumberjack was now rich.
All that wood built our town into this.
The lumberjack worked so hard because he understood,
the tree he cut down was worth the wood!

This Story is a lesson in effort. Read and answer the following questions with friends:

1) Do you think the other lumberjacks were wrong for making fun of him?

2) Why do you think the lumberjack didn't quit?

3) Would you have helped lumberjack chop his tree?

4) Name something you think in your life that is "worth the wood."

5) What has this story taught you?

CPSIA information can be obtained
at www.ICGtesting.com
Printed in the USA
BVHW021914171021
619165BV00001B/3